INSPIRE
CREATIVITY
UNLEASH YOUR IMAGINATION
ANTHOLOGY 2024

INSPIRE CREATIVITY

UNLEASH YOUR IMAGINATION

ANTHOLOGY 2024

COMPILED BY

DEBRA CELOVSKY

Compilation and editing by Debra Celovsky
Final interior copyedit and proofread by Tisha Martin Editorial, LLC
Interior design and layout by Captured By KC Designs
Cover design by Janelle Roselli

ISBN: 978-1-938196-23-2

Printed in the United States of America

Dedication

This anthology is dedicated to all those who willingly offer their creative gifts and further God's kingdom
in countless ways.

It is also dedicated to the members of Inspire Christian Writers who faithfully create work with abilities gifted them by the Holy Spirit. We admire and appreciate you.

For we are his workmanship, created in Christ Jesus for good works, which God prepared ahead of time for us to do.
(Ephesians 2:10 CSB)

Special Thanks to the 2024 Proofreading Team:
Jeanette Breaux, Chris Daniel, Robyn Mulder, Linda Rutzen, Susan Sage, and Adrienne Wartts

Contents

INSPIRE CREATIVITY

UNLEASH YOUR IMAGINATION

ANTHOLOGY 2024

Introduction

In her excellent little book, *Walking on Water*, on Christians and creativity, Madeleine L'Engle writes, "We draw people to Christ not by loudly discrediting what they believe, by telling them how wrong they are and how right we are, but by showing them a light so lovely that they want with all their hearts to know the source of it." This work of "showing a light so lovely" is both our challenge and our delight.

The exercise of our creative gifts comes at a certain cost. That cost is time. We are not assured of any measure of success or acclaim, but we know what we are called to do, and time must be dedicated to that calling. L'Engle quotes the Russian playwright, Anton Chekhov: "You must once and for all give up being worried about successes and failures. Don't let that concern you. It's your duty to go on working steadily day by day, quite quietly, to be prepared for mistakes, which are inevitable, and for failures."

We hope the voices in this year's anthology will encourage you in your own endeavors, and that joy in the giftings of God will permeate all you do.

1

The Blue Elephant

by Debra Celovsky

For years the blue elephant rests in a box along with other childhood treasures until I come across it during one of my decumulating fits. It was created in grade school by my oldest son, Nicolas.

It's quite clever. The large head, with its two pink tusks and curled trunk, is removable, and rests on a round body that sits up, front legs dangling. There are two little eyes, and eyebrows that give him an expression of *Well, let's get going.*

And there is a slit in the top of the head. It is, in fact, an elephant bank. I take it out of the box and display it on a table in the entry of our home. Not long after, Nicolas and his family arrive for dinner and he spies his creation. He picks it up and, with a wry smile says, "I remember that day. Everyone else was making kind of artsy stuff. I sat for a long time looking at my lump of clay and thought, 'It looks like an elephant.' So I made one."

I think about this. He didn't feel pressured or obligated to do what everyone else was doing the way everyone else was doing it. He took the time to see what was really in the clay. And he made the best blue elephant he could make.

What wonderful things would result if we applied those simple decisions to every aspect of our creative endeavors?

C.S. Lewis adds another dimension in considering the creative process. In one of his letters he writes, "'Creation' as applied to human authorship seems to me to be an entirely misleading term. We rearrange elements He has provided. There is not a vestige of real creativity in us . . . because we are recombining elements made by Him and already containing His meanings."

That's a lot to think about on those mornings when I sit looking at a blank screen, waiting for the muse, the vision, the revelation we writers often hope will wash over us in waves of inspiration. Perhaps I should simply sit and ponder—and give thanks for—the inestimable gift of imagination. And I should give thanks as well for the opportunity afforded by our exceedingly generous God to tap the vast riches of his "elements." Then, at some point, I can say to that screen, "God expects you to do your own best today—not somebody else's— with the elements he has made available. And if it looks like an elephant, then that's what it should be."

And it's very likely I'll hear that still, small voice say, *Well, let's get going.*

2

The Memory of You

by Michala Hampton

Sitting cross-legged on my bed, I stare at the empty cardboard boxes hungry to be filled with worldly possessions. A week has passed since Mom dumped them in my room. This morning at breakfast, she threatened to leave everything behind if I didn't finish packing before the movers arrived. Mom never bluffs. I don't care if all my belongings don't make it to the new apartment, but I can't abandon my precious books.

So much for my failed boycott of leaving my childhood home.

I drag my feet over to the bookshelves and start packing my literary treasures. When I reach the bottom shelf containing a variety of leatherbound and spiral notebooks, I pause. I flex my fingers a few times, then plop the notebooks onto my desk.

As I riffle the worn pages, memories flutter through my mind of my adventures with Glezig, the anxious ogre with a phobia of small dogs; Pudding, the pooka, who most enjoyed taking on the form of a dog to scare Glezig; De'Kala, the wise, motherly centaur; and Asha, the adventurous glider, whose imagination soared as high as my own once did.

I scowl and slam the notebooks closed.

Those adventures were over.

The aftermath of a nasty divorce had hardened my mother's heart. Instead of encouraging my writing, she had said my head was in the clouds and I needed to grow up.

My little sister's death forced me to do that.

I grunt and sweep the notebooks into the waste bin.

"What are you doing?" sounds a chirpy voice.

Gasping, I turn toward the window.

Asha perches on the sill. Her sharp talons help her balance. Dark-brown eyes focus intently on me.

My breath catches. I silently berate myself for reminiscing and accidentally summoning one of my characters. I glance around to see if anyone else appears, but they don't. They know they're not welcome—except for Asha. She may be sixteen in glider years, but she looks ten and possesses a childish ignorance I regret writing as one of her traits.

"What are you doing here?" I demand.

"Nice to see you, too, Ren." The layered blue feathers that make up Asha's hair ruffle. She shakes her head, returning the feathers to their smooth, flat position. Asha frowns at the waste bin. "Those don't belong in there."

Heat spreads in my cheeks. Why should I feel embarrassed in front of Asha? She's not real. I clear my throat. "They take up too much space. Besides, Mom and I are moving to a smaller place. I can only take important things."

Asha's feathered brow furrows. "Those notebooks are important."

"Not anymore. I'm seventeen and have no more time for childish fantasies." Under my breath, I mutter, "It's time for me to grow up."

Her feathers ruffle again. She purses her pale blue lips in disapproval.

Ignoring her, I resume packing my books.

Asha jumps off the windowsill, rustling her leafy attire, and strides toward the waste bin. She stares at the notebooks. "You used to love writing, especially for—"

"Don't," I warn. Over this past year, I've developed a sense for recognizing when people are about to say my sister's name. My therapist insists I should speak it, because its very meaning is life.

Speaking life won't bring my little sister back.

"You're acting like she doesn't exist anymore." Asha crosses her arms. "Like us."

I glare. "She doesn't. She's dead."

A purple blush appears on Asha's light-blue cheeks. "Her memory is alive, but you're trying to toss it away like those notebooks."

"That's enough!"

"I remember that day. I remember how it felt." Asha clenches her jaw. "The pain—real pain—of losing someone I love."

"You don't know anything about loss or grief." I slam a book. "You're not made of flesh and blood."

Asha's warbling pitch grows higher and sharper. "No, but you still gave me a heart because you poured yours into creating me!"

I roll my eyes. "And you've brought me nothing but grief."

Asha stomps her foot. "Grief is why you started writing in the first place!"

Fighting against a shudder, I try to speak, but my words don't come as naturally as they did when I used to write. Tears fall from Asha's eyes. I blink away the moisture gathering in my own. I refuse to cry. But Asha has no shame. She wears her heart on her sleeve like my sister did.

"You wrote to help both of you escape the pain of your parents' divorce," Asha continues. "Glezig, Pudding, De'Kala, me—all of us were born out of your grief."

"Stop!" I command.

"Now you're stuck in two worlds where you can't escape your pain, so you've stopped writing about it in our world, but choose not to face it in your own."

I grit my teeth. "Be quiet."

"Why won't you write anymore?" Asha shakes her head in dismay. "Why would you give life to me and the others just to throw us away?"

The answer forms on my tongue, but I bite down hard. Asha can't know the truth.

As she studies me, her eyes widen. "You blame me, don't you? If I hadn't flown across the street, she wouldn't have followed and—" Asha covers her mouth with one hand. "I–I'm sorry."

Grief hits me as hard as the car must have hit my sister. I grip the back of my desk chair, taking strained breaths. "I don't blame you."

"Yes, you do."

"No!" I swipe a whole shelf of books onto the floor, scattering them. "I wrote those stupid stories with all of you stupid characters. I lived in your world and she joined me." My voice cracks. "I killed her." I slump down to the floor and bury my head in my hands, sobbing. It takes me a few minutes to speak again in a strained voice. "Mom and everyone else know she loved pretending to be the hero with all of you. They know it's my fault, and that's why—" I squeeze my eyes and tremble.

"That's why you can't say her name," Asha finished. "You think it will dishonor her memory."

I wince and give a shaky nod.

A taloned hand rests on my knee. I lift my head and meet Asha's warm, compassionate gaze.

"You wrote because it brought healing. Words heal." She gives my knee an affectionate squeeze. "I'm not real, so you're safe. You can speak her name to me."

I inhale a sharp breath.

"What's your sister's name, Ren?" Asha asks softly.

The name tangles with a lump in my throat. Dryness forms in my mouth as I try to speak. After several moments, I swallow hard and whisper, "Vivian."

Asha nods and grimaces. "Please don't let me die. When Vivian passed, we lost a piece of you. And the day you stopped writing, we all lost a piece of ourselves." Her eyes mist again. "If you throw away those notebooks, we will all die."

Goosebumps spring up on my arms. I rub at them and regard Asha with tenderness. My sister was my inspiration for this sweet character, and she had loved Asha as much as I had loved Vivian.

If Asha ceases to exist, then my sister's memory really will be gone.

I can't allow Vivian to die a second death.

Pushing to my feet, I hurry over to the waste bin and retrieve the notebooks. I close my eyes and cradle them against my chest. The memories of my beloved characters flood me, but this time I don't shut them out. I look up and offer Asha an apologetic smile.

She swipes her arm across her damp face. Her lips twitch

upward. "Don't forget why you started writing."

I stiffen and clutch the notebooks tighter.

Asha scurries to the window and climbs out onto the roof. The tattooed wings on her back manifest into a real pair. Childish mischief gleams in her eyes. "When you finish the chapter about me and Pooka crossing Viper Canyon, tell Jack about it."

I cock my head. "The boy across the street?"

"That's the one." Her bright, youthful expression becomes solemn. "You didn't give Vivian death. You gave her hope, and she shared it with Jack. Keep writing for both of them."

My jaw drops, and Asha's blue form shimmers.

She winks and soars away.

I glance at my notebooks, scribbled with hope and life. The reason I started writing was to escape my grief. The magic of the world and characters I created had brought unexpected healing to me and Vivian. Without her, the magic was gone.

Could it ever be revived?

Only one way to find out.

Wiping away my tears, I sit at my desk, open a notebook to a blank page, and pick up a pen.

3

A Creative Heart Held in God's Hands

by Kimberly Novak

> **But now, Lord, You are our Father;**
> **We are the clay, and You our potter,**
> **And all of us are the work of Your hand.**
> **(Isaiah 64:8 NASB)**

What did I get myself into? A question I've asked a million times. I have a knack for putting myself in situations where I feel ill-equipped. I'm unsure why it happens, but when it comes to something creative, there is a side of me that enjoys being outside my comfort zone. It's as if the attraction taps into the imaginative side of my brain, and I can't resist.

As a writer, I use words to create a world of imagination, inspiration, and education. So, how did I end up at an art retreat? The attractive photo and clever wording on the website drew me in, but the nudges of my creative heart calling me into a new level of relationship with God and prayer made me sign up.

Even when the what did I get myself into thoughts bubbled up, I committed to going outside myself and allowing God to mold me in new ways. I held my fingers over the keyboard, cling-ing to sayings like, "If God brings you to it, he will bring you through it," and "Why not give in to abandon and allow the Holy Spirit to guide?" Then, I hit the register button, and the rest is history!

I have attended Creative Expression for Spiritual Growth four times. Every year, my objective is the same: incorporate the fruits of my art experiences into my writing practice. The first year, my plan didn't seem so bright once I realized I had to produce art through drawing, collage, and painting.

Oh, how I longed for my keyboard and the ability to be creative through the written word. Having committed to the three-day experience, I set aside my inhibitions and allowed God to take over. I knew I had to get out of my head and into my heart. After all, God sent me there, and I couldn't let him down.

At that first retreat, I learned many things about myself and how God and I communicate through creativity. I also became educated on my emotional expression of specific artistic abilities. For instance, I cannot look away from the paper and draw the face of the person seated across from me. My likeness of her fails to capture her true beauty. I can, however, use colors and brush-strokes to convey felt emotions. These are emotions I never knew existed. As I delve into the artistic moment, I enter into creative dialogue with God to talk through the feelings as they arise.

Water has always brought me spiritual comfort, and painting with watercolors reminds me of the peace God brings. I get the most pleasure from flicking the paint off the brush onto the paper and letting the paint dots create a heavenly surprise. However, I quickly learned that my table partner did not appreciate the glorious splatter coming from my side of the table. I reminded her that we were supposed to create what makes us happy. Apparently, for me, that's splattering paint.

During the most recent retreat, the instruction penetrated deeper into my soul. On day one I realized that art and spirituality spring forth from God's love. The mere fact that I am created in God's image and that God loves me is enough to keep my heart connected to any creative work God may be calling me toward. I fully comprehended that I am not just mixing paints when I create. I am mixing my soul with God.

Looking back, I see many differences in myself from the first year I attended to the most recent. First of all, I actually hung the canvas I painted on my office wall this year. I love looking at it and remembering how close I felt to God as the paint soaked into the canvas. In previous years, the artwork found its home in a box buried deep within the confines of my closet. No one else needed to see that. This year was different because I focused so much on creating with God that I could see his influence in the brush strokes and color choices.

This year's reflective talks also touched me significantly because they focused on elements of the brain and trusting yourself through God's guidance. These topics were essential for me as I had survived a traumatic brain injury only five months prior. I knew the retreat was a godsend when the speaker said, "Despite where you are and what you are going through, God will get you through." I'm not usually big on asking God to send little signs or confirmations that I made the correct choice. However, given the circumstances of my injury, this one brought my hand to my heart. Since then, when I feel my heartbeat, I remind myself that in every heartbeat is the heartbeat of God!

The insights and discussion on the brain focused on how

the two hemispheres relate to creativity. The left brain is the data center. People who function from this side of the brain are math wizards, scientists, and the like. Definitely not me! Math and I do not coexist. The right brain is the creative side, where artists like me are more comfortable. Then, there is the golden brain, living between both brains and, ironically, where my brain injury occurred. God gave us both sides of the brain and wants us to use them to our full potential. People who live on one side of the brain have a yearning for the other side, and that is why I sign up for things that bring me out of my comfort zone. Who knew?

Since my injury, I honestly feel like I'm living in someone else's brain. I surprised myself when I realized that the colors I used in the past to emote joy, grace, and peace, had changed. In the first year of the retreat, these colors were various blues and yellows. Now, they come through in pinks and greens. Not only that, but the brushstrokes tell a different story. I have gone from short, wavy lines to long, flared-out lines, allowing me to create artistic renderings differently. It's as if my brain has finally surrendered to how God wants to use my creative tendencies.

I'll never know if the changes stem from the injury to the brain or God's transformative powers each year I have attended the retreat. All that matters is how I carry on what I have learned, and lean into God's gentle hands leading the way.

At the retreat's conclusion, I was sent forth to proclaim the glory of God through my creativity. I have made a concerted effort to bring God into everything I do, especially my creative works. Specifically, I must begin spiritual writing with prayer and Scripture to have a consecrated pen. I cannot expect God to bless my hands if I have not invited him on the journey.

On the spiritual side of creativity, by incorporating how God and I interact through the process of art, I open myself up to hearing God's Word in new ways. Scripture teaches me to pray without ceasing. The art retreat teaches me to allow prayer to guide my hands and thinking. God, spirituality, and art become one with practice, commitment, and consistency.

I have learned to let it go when I hold back on my creative side. I know that by using my gifts and talents, I am working with God, and God is working through me. I am a true artist when I allow my brain to be flexible and go wild. As I create, communication between God and me becomes apparent as I acknowledge what happens internally and externally. For instance, when I flick the paint off the brush and watch it land on the paper, I cannot help but smile, and my heart becomes that of a little girl walking in faith.

Most importantly, I let God show me the art, then sit back and be open to what God wants me to see. At first glance, the canvas may look like a hot mess! When I close my eyes and look again through the eyes of faith, with a heart yearning for my Creator, I will look upon a priceless masterpiece.

The experience of the retreat has shown me that I didn't "get myself into anything." God placed me right where he knew I needed to be so I could become the artist he made me to be. When I weave new artistic skills into spiritual writing, I awaken parts of me that may have been buried or forgotten about. I see actual images now when writing, even though I only put words on paper. Vivid colors and majestic scenery become alive, all because I allow my creative heart to be held in God's hands.

4

Time Left to Squeeze Out Love

by Joyce D. Hightower

Sally hung up the phone with a heavy heart. A close family friend, Dr. David Green, had called to warn her of the bad news he had just given Arnie, her husband. The biopsy was positive. The cancer had returned. Although the news made her dizzy, she took a deep breath and started planning. She'd always been good at that. Now more than ever, she must be ready to support Arnie when he arrived from his clinic appointment.

It would be best, she thought, if Arnie found her busy when he entered the house. It would help hide her grief about David's warning and help calm her pounding heart and trembling hands. She mixed a small casserole and placed it in the oven. Then she bustled into the dining room and set the stage for her plan on the table. She set up craft materials, tools, and project supplies at the far end. At the other end, she hurried to set two places for lunch.

Sally jumped, startled at the sound of Arnie's car in the driveway. Clenching her fists, she froze to keep from running to hug him close. The front door clicking closed was followed by keys tossed on the foyer table.

"Sally, I'm home," his voice called down the hall.

Allowing herself to move again, she replied, "I'm in the dining room getting lunch ready to serve. Wash up and come have a seat." She finished putting the plates and cutlery in place.

There was no verbal reply. But hearing water running in the guest bathroom let her know he had heard. The tinkle of ice in the water glasses greeted Arnie's appearance at the hall door. A frown of question spread over his tired face. "All this for sandwiches?"

"No, I've prepared something special. I'm trying out a new casserole recipe I plan to take to the women's meeting this weekend. I figure if you like it, they will love it." She leaned forward to receive his kiss on her cheek.

"I'm a guinea pig again? At least you're a good cook," he said, sitting at the head of the table.

Sally watched out of the corner of her eye as he fiddled with his napkin. They both seemed intent on avoiding eye contact. Their dance of words around the wretched news continued.

"I'll be right back," she said, hurrying to the kitchen. Safely inside, she took another deep breath. "Oh, no, you don't," she said to the lump beginning to form in her throat. She looked at her reflection in the oven door window and formed a smile. Armed with oven mittens, she carried the dish to the table and cut the contents into neat squares to help it cool and serve better.

They held hands as Arnie blessed the food. He dished a helping onto his plate and opened his mouth wide for a big first bite.

Sally glanced at his face for his verdict as she served her plate. "That was quite a mouthful just to taste something." She watched him chew and then prepare to take another mouthful. "Wait. Tell me what you think?"

"After seeing the broccoli pieces, it's more delicious than I expected."

"Thank you. That's a green light for the women's meeting." Tasting it, she agreed. "It is good."

"So, what's all that at the other end of the table?" He pointed with his fork to the craft supplies.

"Oh, that's a surprise I want you to help me with after lunch. It's been so handy having you around since you retired. Had I known you had such a good eye for design and color, I would have put you to work years ago."

In a reverent tone, Arnie closed his eyes and said, "Dear Lord, thank you for letting my artistic genius remain undiscovered until after I left my other job." He peeked at her through one half-opened eye. Then, he took another bite.

"You're so funny, Arnie. As I said, I need your help making a card for each of our grandchildren. I was thinking—" Sally took deep breaths, looking down at her plate, trying to regain control.

Arnie finished chewing and put his fork down. He gazed at her, then grasped and squeezed her hand. Closing his eyes, he sighed and whispered, "David Green called you, didn't he?"

"Yes," she croaked.

"Come on, Sally. Please don't look at me with that distress. Cover our plates. We can reheat the food later. Let's see what you've got over there."

Making their way to the other end of the table, Sally explained, "I thought you would enjoy making cards for each of our grandchildren. You can choose a theme and create a poem or note you want. While I'm typing it out, you can pick cutouts of their favorite toys or things. Let your inspiration flow."

"Okay, we'll see how it goes."

"How did you come up with this? It's a great idea. I haven't even thought of my cancer for the last hour." Arnie smiled, looking at his watch.

"I know that when you create and design beautiful things for those you love, the world becomes brighter and full of joy."

"I can imagine God dancing joyfully during the first six days of creation."

"You know, honey, I can see that too," she laughed.

"We can do this faster if we separate all the girls' and boys' stuff so I have a clear idea of my choices. There," he said, rearranging some of the cutouts over the card's front surface. "You see? The flower can be down here. I'll draw these curved lines on either side, making it look like it is blowing in the breeze." He sketched the lines described with a marker.

"That was a beautiful touch," Sally declared.

"Great. Let's do the next one. This will be for Tommy."

"Okay, but we need to take a break. Can you believe we have been working for hours? I'll heat the food and be right back."

She placed the warm plates on the table in minutes and returned to stand by Arnie. "It's ready. Let me see what you've done." Lifting the card, she smiled, "This is the best one so far. Maybe I'm holding you back. You're doing wonderfully without me."

"I'll never do better without your help. This was your idea, after all."

"But you brought it to life. Can we talk about the melanoma popping up again after three years of disappearing? Can't something be done? Tell me everything, starting with last week's appointment."

Arnie reviewed, thinking he had strained his shoulder while gardening in the backyard. When he went to see his doctor, a look of concern clouded Dr. David Green's usual composure. A feeling of dread chilled him as the doctor sat heavily on the chair in the exam room. It was an enlarged lymph node, a new finding. With Arnie's history of cancer, they needed a needle biopsy of the node and some other blood tests as well. The testing was arranged on an urgent basis for the following day.

"I went with you for that biopsy," Sally said. "I was looking forward to hearing the results today."

"Look, I went to today's results appointment alone. That was selfish. But it was so I could focus on the results without worrying about your reaction. You're the strong one, you know. Anyway, the cancer has spread to other places. An appointment with a specialist is set to hear treatment options."

"And . . .?"

"David said the worst-case scenario is a quick decline and death in six to ten months. So, if God decides that the best thing for us is not to heal me, we have to finish this project soon. Then we'll try to complete any other creation we can squeeze into the time available."

Sally's eyes teared. "Okay. Let's eat, and then get this show on the road. We have a lot of praying, phoning, and card-making to do. Maybe you can make cards for the upcoming holidays. You could make a short storybook and send a copy to each grandchild. Don't forget to write a letter to their parents, our children."

"Yes, all good ideas. We have to get busy. I'll bring more stacks of magazines from the garage for cutouts."

"Wait. Let's eat first. The food will get cold again."

"It'll only take a second. I just thought of a funny theme for Thanksgiving," Arnie called, rushing down the hall, whistling.

Sally whispered into the silence, "Lord, keep the ideas coming. It's such a joy to let creativity be fueled by love and to produce beautiful fruit. May it ripple through Arnie into lives around him for a long time."

5

C-R-E-A-T-I-V-E

by Maureen Miller

**Make a careful exploration of who you are and the work you
have been given, and then sink yourself into that. Don't be
impressed with yourself. Don't compare yourself with others.
Each of you must take responsibility for doing the creative best
you can with your own life.**
(Galatians 6:4–5 MSG)

As a creative, it's my aim to live with eyes and ears open. I
desire to see and hear God in his created world, experiencing him in the people, places, objects, and circumstances each day
presents.

Take, for example, life on our family farm. I might see and
hear God's creativity in the bellow of our Scottish Highland cattle.
I may sense him in the giggles of my grandgirls. I can savor his
creativity in the sweetness of blueberries freshly picked from the
bush.

Having experienced God, I express my thoughts and feelings
in my particular artistic form, through written words. Not gifted
with a painter's palette or a lump of clay on the potter's wheel, my
experiences translate themselves as words on the page. Sometimes

they're simply for me; other times, for a broader audience.

Personally, I find fulfillment in painting pictures with words, similar to the satisfaction I imagine for those who paint with oils or watercolors. Like other artistic forms, writing is an outpouring of my gratitude, a means of inner healing, and an expression of other emotion.

Pondering my particular form of creativity led me to consider the word "creative" as an acrostic. Taking each letter, I've chosen a theme upon which to expound. My aim? To paint with words, pointing readers to the creative nature of God and his Son—the one another creative of long ago a storyteller named John referred to as The Word.

<u>C is for children.</u> As a mother and grandmother, I can't remember a time I didn't love and appreciate little humans. From an early age, when I'd play with dolls, dreaming of becoming a momma, until the present, I take pleasure in children. It was no surprise when I chose elementary education as a career, teaching students from tiny toddlers to blossoming boys and girls in their last year of grade school.

From freckle-faced redheads to blue-eyed blondes, children come in all shapes and sizes, with varying skin tones and personalities. They remind us of God's creativity in their unique laughter, as well as in their preferences.

It's no surprise the Creator chose to redeem the world by sending his Son, and Jesus didn't arrive as a full-grown man, but as a baby, growing from boyhood to become an adult. Like my grandgirls, God's Son, too, probably loved to make mud pies, pick wildflowers, and savor a strawberry's sweetness.

<u>R is for relationship.</u> Though an introvert, I love and appreciate people. Whether I'm with children or adults who happen to be family members, friends, or strangers, my relationships matter. Not only do I pray to make a positive difference in people's lives, I know others make a difference in mine as well. Sometimes another's impact is good, sometimes negative. This is the reason we're encouraged in God's Word to choose our close relationships with care.

Jesus modeled the importance of relationship through his choosing of twelve, somewhat rough-and-tumble, disciples. Think of the variations of these men. From methodical tax collector Levi (a.k.a. Matthew) to fiery, passionate Simon (a.k.a. Peter), each was made in God's image. They were an expression of the Creator's creativity, and their individual and corporate relationship with Jesus during his three years of ministry was unique and important.

E is for elderly. These impactful humans are beautiful examples of God's creative handiwork. Just sit a spell with someone whose experiences span more than seven or eight decades. He or she once knew nothing of texting, emojis, or Facetime, and survived without the convenience of fast food, email, and AI. Ingenuity and creativity were essential, out of which were born corn cob dolls and paper airplanes.

As varied as their physical appearance, each elderly person, created in God's beautiful image, possesses a treasure trove of personal experiences. We can learn from each one, even if the lessons learned are what not to do, how not to live. The aged are a unique bunch, and I appreciate the wealth of wisdom the elderly offer, if only I take time to listen and observe.

A is for animal. Imagine the Garden of Eden on the day

God spoke fish, birds, and land creatures into existence. With their arrival came new colors, textures, sounds, and scents. From the porcupine to the platypus, the parrot to the peacock, the puffer to the piranha, animals added so much to our world, and this planet has never been the same.

How fun it must have been for Adam and Eve to name them, then care for the animals. Personally, I believe heaven will be filled with these creatures, each in its perfected state. After all, don't we read the lion will lie at peace with the lamb?

T is for taste. Another gift from the Creator, something introduced from the beginning in the Garden, is food. The abundance of flavors that we taste are part of God's creative plan. From sour to sweet, tangy to spicy, there's no end to the tastes we can experience. Indeed, we are the recipients of God's culinary creativity.

As foodies, my husband and I enjoy trying a variety of ethnic foods. From Japanese sushi, with a touch of wasabi, ginger, and soy sauce, to down-home, freshly cranked peach ice cream, each tantalizes our taste buds. And God, in his creativity, made our tongues with sections perfectly designed for tasting, to differentiate between bitter, sour, salty, and sweet.

I is for invention. From the beginning of time, God set the example by inventing. First, after sin entered the world, God took the life of an animal. Then, in his mercy, he used the pelt to fashion clothing for Adam and Eve.

Throughout history humans have applied their God-given creativity to invent. In ancient times, stone tools, bricks, wheels, and papyrus were imagined into existence. Later, there was paper, then printing methods. More recently, the atomic bomb, hovercrafts, and cancer immunotherapy have been invented.

There's simply no end to what men, women, and children will think up as they live out their God-given creativity. As long as humans have imagination, until Jesus returns and perhaps even after, there will be new ideas birthed to become great inventions.

V is for villain. As a creative wordsmith, one who loves good story, villains, also called antagonists, are integral. They keep us on the edges of our seats and give us a reason to cheer.

From the beginning, in the greatest story ever told, the Bible, there have been villains. First was a cunning serpent. Generations later, a band of jealous, cruel brothers dumped Joseph in a pit, which led to his introduction to Potiphar's seductive wife. David met, then killed, a pompous giant named Goliath. And how about the New Testament, with sinister King Herod? And let's not forget Judas Iscariot who, with a twist of irony, betrayed our Savior with a kiss.

But what about figurative villains? Even for creatives there are meddling antagonists. For the photographer, it's poor lighting; the painter, a dismal day; the potter, high humidity.

Though they may be irritating, even dangerous, at times, villains are part of our stories—again, until Jesus returns. But unlike the possibility of new inventions, there will be no antagonists in heaven.

E is for ever. Because we're each creatives, designed by the Creator to create, and because my outlet is story, this last letter reminds me of the final two words in most fairytales—ever after. Usually this follows the word "happily," as in happily ever after.

We are amply familiar with the truth that happily ever after is not, at least for now, our experience. We and those we love face illness, sometimes unto death. Jobs are lost. Children rebel. Pets run away. Crops fail. Money runs out. That is a plain, hard fact.

The word "ever" is defined as at all times; always. There's only one thing which satisfies this definition—only one who ever and always will ever and always.

He's the author of our unique and creative stories, no matter how much pain and imperfection might pepper our years, destroy our days, mess with our minutes, and sabotage our seconds.

Because the right now is yet unfamiliar with our future perfection. But one day?

And behold, I am coming quickly, and My reward is with Me, to give every one according to his work. I am the Alpha and the Omega, the Beginning and the End, the First and the Last. (Revelation 22:12–13 NKJV)

Indeed, our happily ever after is coming. So, create on, creatives. Create on.

6

Created to Create

by Dian Avila

Offshore, smooth liquid sapphire

Arcs keep on rising.

The crown curls under.

Emerald light pierces the crest.

Billions of diamonds bounce, fade,

And scatter on shore.

The next azure swell

Shows sparks of aquamarine,

Before dissolving on sand,

Displaying God's creation.

A captivating plot arc
Tugs at the reader
As the conflict peaks.
We stare at sure disaster
Rescued by character growth.
God's truth is revealed.
Rough refined diamonds
Shine into reality.
A glint of truth resounding
By his child's creation.

A carved, colorful canyon
Displays rocks and soil,
Paints a mosaic.
Sunlight dances around clouds
Creating tapestry hues:
Lime, navy, auburn,
Amber, coral, red,
Burgundy, mahogany,
And cobalt-pearl waterfalls.
God's elegance is displayed.

A hustling concrete jungle
Flaunts his masterpieces.
The city displays
Creators, imitators,
Coders, writers, artists, dads,
Dancers, singers, moms,
Colored like canyons.
He molds us to live in light.
Crafted to be like Jesus,
Created we create.

7

Journey to Creativity

by Libby Taylor-Worden

OK! I admit it. I'm more comfortable as a plotter than a pantser both in non-fiction and fiction. And I'm not ashamed of it. But it wasn't always that way.

I used to think my sisters were the creative ones in the family. Crafts, knitting, quilting, sewing, and baking were just some of their specialties. They won blue ribbons at the fair for everything from a macramé chair to peanut butter cheesecake. I'm the one who declared, "I don't do baking," the way a professional house-keeper might include the caveat, "I don't do windows."

In fact, during sister retreats, I would sequester myself in a quiet bedroom so I could work on writing project while my sisters listened to books on tape as they quilted. My perception was, they expressed creativity in quilts while I just worked. I wasn't convinced the mental effort to write curriculum for Sunday school classes, magazine articles, or blog posts was an expression of creativity.

Once I asked Joyce, my younger sister, to help paint my bathroom. I'd spent hours taping off everything I didn't want painted—like mirrors, tile, fixtures, and hinges. Joyce grabbed a roller when she arrived and asked, "Where do I start?"

"Wait a minute." I began to shake. "Let me just add a row of paint around all the tape and then you can take a roller to the walls."

Joyce just poured paint into the tray, soaked the roller, and went at it. With a one-inch brush I tried to stay ahead of her. I began with the space above the door that was the biggest candidate for getting paint on the ceiling. Painting as fast as I could, I tried to keep up.

She left two hours later with a two-inch border between the rolled paint and the tape. I finished hours later having painted all day with my one-inch brush. In the years since, we've often laughed about it, admitting that the world needs both rollers and one-inch brushes. Still, I didn't see myself as a creative person. Joyce was the just-do-it type, and I was precision.

Tongue in cheek, I often declared, "I don't have a right side to my brain."

Then one day I took a right brain/left brain self-assessment and discovered I'm smack dab in the middle of the spectrum. This made me research right- and left-brain functions and their influence on creativity. I discovered both sides have the capacity for creative expression.

The right brain is more loosely defined, free-flowing. Right-brainers color outside the lines. They are more fluid, less planning. They may even change directions midstream. They plan as they go—like grabbing a roller to start painting before the borders are defined. Some decidedly right-brain painters were impressionists like Monet, Picasso, Renoir, and van Gogh.

Left-brained creativity is more likely to spawn precision. These artists include architects, electrical panel designers, mind-mappers, illustrators, and yes, painters. Left-brain painting examples most notably include portraiture, but can be landscape and still life. Some left-brain painters' works resemble photographs. These artists include Rosa Bonheur, Edouard Manet, Gustave Courbet, and Norman Rockwell.

Like any muscle, however, creativity needs practice to develop. I first started writing by dreaming. That's right, daydreaming. It got me in trouble as a young girl but, over time, evolved into dreaming of becoming a writer because of the stories in my head. Occasionally I'd write down ideas for books. Eventually a few ideas turned into book outlines, but then I filed them away. My reasoning was I gave all my imaginative energy to my eight-to-five job. I know—an excuse.

At work one day, I wrote a piece for a trade journal. Another time, an article for a women's magazine. It was quite a thrill to realize others saw my writing as worthy of publishing. Eventually I began to develop curriculum for a Sunday school class I was teaching.

The turning point in recognizing my own aptitude for creativity was when I wrote a letter. A man at church sitting a few rows ahead of me laid his head on his wife's shoulder and his back heaved with uncontrollable shaking. It was Dean, my Sunday school teacher. I later discovered his son had committed suicide just days before. I didn't know his son. I barely knew Dean. Yet I felt called to write him a letter. Never having been a parent, I questioned whether I was qualified to write to him at all—but I couldn't dismiss the weight of the calling.

I struggled with how to begin, but then it started to flow. After three pages of handwritten words, I reread the first draft. I was surprised how obvious it was to distinguish my words from God's inspired words. I drew a line about four inches down from the top of the first page where God's message to Dean kicked in. Then I rewrote the letter from that point.

It was a moment I'll never forget. I felt like a pen as God's ink flowed through me. The confirmation came over a year later when I learned Dean had kept that letter and reread it repeatedly. God could communicate to others in their distress through my willingness to sit down and pick up a pen. I had nothing in particular to say. It was merely my willingness to be used.

Was this creativity? I wanted to do it again and again. But God doesn't work on cue.

Fast-forward a few years. Attending my first writer's conference, I took an Easter pageant screenplay as my work-in-progress for a workshop. Our first exercise was to add drama to heighten the tension between key characters. But my key characters were God the Father, Jesus, and the Holy Spirit.

"You need to come up with another topic," the workshop leader whispered as he walked behind my chair.

I had one minute. It occurred to me I should write about what I know—not an original thought, but certainly good advice. Then it came to me. I minister with my husband to the black-leather, often referred to as "outlaw," motorcycle world. So, I began writing in that workshop about the motorcycle culture.

I had just been dabbling in a screenplay, so fiction was completely foreign to me. I knew less about writing fiction than how to write a letter. But I started anyway. This did not turn the fiction-writing creativity faucet on in my brain, however.

It made me ponder: Should you take a creative person and

teach them the craft? Or, is it better to start with someone in the field of writing and exercise their creativity muscle? These musings brought to mind an interview team at work where we debated: "Should we hire a subject-matter expert and teach them how to design curriculum, or do we take an instructional technologist and introduce them to the content?" You got it. I was the lone instructional technologist on the team of subject-matter experts. I felt like a fish swimming upstream trying to extol the value of developing learning objectives before the training materials.

Still not convinced I was creative, I set a goal to learn to write fiction. After all, I was in-between left- and right-brained ability, I had the desire, and I was successful at various other forms of writing. I'd been told it was about a ten-year learning curve to write fiction well. Workshops, critique groups, conferences, books on craft, and hours of writing and rewriting were the steps it took to sharpen creativity and tap into God's inspired voice to produce fiction others wanted to read.

My journey began with a dream, then I recognized God's inspiration as part of the process. I'd already written magazine articles, graduated to curricula, launched a blog, dabbled in anthologies, was a published journalist, and then wrote a nonfiction book. Following the passion for fiction that surfaced within me, I trusted God would facilitate the learning curve and use me to send a message to others through the stories in my head.

Am I famous? Not one bit. "Don't quit your day job" was the best advice I received at my first writers conference twenty-six years ago. Is my writing effective? Occasional feedback confirms that it is. I believe there was a purpose for God to bestow on me the desire to write.

Instead of measuring my success in conventional ways, I rely on God's promise:

I planted, Apollos watered, but God was causing the growth. So then neither the one who plants nor the one who waters is anything, but God who causes the growth.
(I Corinthians 3:6–7 NASB)

Today my experience of creativity can best be summed up in a few words adapted from an Academy Award-winning screenplay by Colin Welland for the movie, *Chariots of Fire*:

"When I write, I feel his glory."

8

The Flowers' Spring Performance

by Ellie Langford

The flowers take center stage.
Spotlighted by sunbeams, they gracefully sway.
The wind gently ruffles their petal dresses.
Some are soft, dreamy pastels
and others are bold, flaming colors.
Admirers, the young and the old,
enjoy the ever-changing, creative performance.
Soon the flowers slip away from the stage,
first one . . . then another . . . 'til all are gone.
Not wanting it to end and longing for more,
several fans shout, "Encore! Encore!"
The more experienced fans reply,
"The Creator will present many more
beautiful, inspiring performances."

9

The Blank Page

by Robyn Mulder

You can't edit a blank page. I've heard that sentence many times over the years as I've attended writing conferences. Of course, it's true. Writers have to get words written onto a page or typed into a document if they want to see a project come to completion. Even if those words make no sense at first, they must be poured out through pencil lead, ink, or typing fingers. Once the words are on the page they can be examined, deleted, manipulated, and polished to become a creative work of art.

In my head, I know this. So why do I usually procrastinate and wait until inspiration (or a looming deadline) prompts me to write? I find distractions and excuses that keep me from working on the projects filling my mind. The blank page scares me, and I avoid it at all costs. Once I do start writing, my efforts are often rushed, and there is a sense of pressure as I pour out my thoughts.

Usually, the finished piece is pretty good, and this just exacerbates the problem. *I work best under pressure* becomes my mantra, and the cycle is repeated.

I don't want to keep living that way. God has blessed me with creative talents, and I want to use them for his glory. He is, after all, a supremely creative God. He created all of the unique plants, animals, and humans on this earth, not to mention the amazing bodies of water and landscapes that we can appreciate for all of their beauty.

***For we are God's handiwork, created in Christ Jesus to do good works, which God prepared in advance for us to do.*
(Ephesians 2:10 NIV)**

That verse can inspire our creativity, if we let it. God created us, and he has plans for us to bless others with the good works he wants us to do. Some people sew, others bake, while others can paint or draw. Musicians use their creativity to compose and play inspiring or comforting songs. Writers create pages and pages of resources that educate, inspire, challenge, and entertain.

None of those blessings can happen if the sewer doesn't sew, the baker doesn't bake, the painter doesn't paint, the musician doesn't play, and the writer doesn't write. And, unfortunately, there are so many writers who don't write. That blank page mocks them and they do whatever they can to get away from it.

Our thoughts about the blank page matter. When we look at that empty space, it can be daunting. Negative thoughts will bring fear, uncertainty, and paralysis. Thinking about future criticisms and rejections can stifle our creativity. We consider all of the possible negative outcomes of our work and we do anything we can to avoid even getting started.

What if we try to think more positively about the blank page? What if we focus on all of the glorious possibilities that empty space presents? What if we let ourselves wonder about the possible outcomes once we make the decision to fill that page with words?

No pressure. No expectations. No preconceived notions. Just a curious excitement about what could result if we pour out our words on that blank page. Creativity will bubble up from our very souls if we allow our words to flow freely.

We need to just start writing, whether it's on a piece of paper or in a document on our computer. We can't wait until inspiration strikes or the deadline approaches. We can't let ourselves question anything. Let's just get the words out. No self-editing. No self-doubt. No self-judgment.

Once the stream of thoughts is down on paper or captured in a document, then we can slow down and play with them. Rearrange, replace, rewrite—artistically organizing it all to create something beautiful.

I'm going to practice developing my creativity by bravely filling the blank page, and I hope you will too.

There's no telling what your words will become. A poem, an essay, a blog post, a short story, a nonfiction book, a memoir, a novel? Who knows? Whatever it turns out to be, it will be proof of your creativity. There's no creativity in the blank page!

10

Resurrected Art

by Carlitta Cole-Kelly

One man carried a shotgun, the other a hatchet and a pistol. Neither of them knew what they would find inside the old wooden house. It had become little more than an empty edifice where the walls told sad truths or lies that death could neither refute nor affirm—not without written proof anyway. At least, this was the scene I imagined when Zeb told me about the weapons they took with them that day—and what they found inside.

"What? No way!" I exclaimed to my cousin Zebedee as he shared via phone about their foray into his grandfather, Henry's, abandoned house in rural Alabama. It had been many years since his last visit to the house he grew up in with his late mother and her father. There had not been any reason to go back.

Zeb and I had met via genealogical research and a subsequent family reunion in 2003, just a few years prior to his return trip that day. I had urged him to go sooner to look around for old photos, books, or treasures that might breathe new life into the story of our lost familial ties. It was several more years before he finally decided to return, coaxing a friend along to battle the high weeds outside, and poisonous snakes or rodent squatters they might find inside.

I could hardly contain myself once Zeb confirmed there were indeed relatives' letters amid old farm ledgers buried under thick layers of dust and dirt.

"I can't believe how well my grandfather kept records about everything," Zeb said. "Look, I'm going to copy the letters and send them to you soon as I can."

I nodded on the other end of the phone as if he could see me 2,051 miles away. I inhaled deeply, then exhaled, hoping to release all the angst of mail delivery—and the time it would take for the letters to reach me on the West Coast.

Once the letters arrived, I sat like a bookworm in the corner of my bedroom, ingesting every nutrient-rich word, syllable, and inflection of speech. The one from my late grandmother, dated April 9, 1944, was the most meaningful. She was the woman who blessed my life early on, teaching me at a young age about Jesus and how to say my nighttime prayers and bless my food.

My grandmother had written to her first cousin, Martha, Henry's sister, about her life and work in neighboring Mississippi. She mentioned the recent heavy rains, the high cost of fifteen-cent sweet milk, and her parents' well-being, peppering other details with a bit of gossip. She hoped to see her cousin Martha again one day, and suggested that the accompanying picture she had drawn be kept for "as long as you can."

I had always known about my grandmother's creative abilities since I had grown up watching her. Known to be a soul food artisan, she was also quick to doodle, sew, and crochet. Later, she had begun painting ceramics at her senior citizen classes.

But in 1944, just before the final year of World War II, she had sat down to create a crude black-and-white pencil drawing on regular lined paper. It was of two soldiers in dress uniform standing at attention while singing. The soldiers' closed eyes displayed thick lashes, their lips the color of lead, and they held a hymnbook in their hands. Above the soldiers' heads, in the top left corner of the page, was a bust of Jesus wearing a robe, the folds of the garment covering his chest and shoulders. Beside him was a square sign with the words, "The Tomb, He Arose."

Undoubtedly, Resurrection Sunday had been a focus at the time of her April letter. So with Jesus on her mind and inspired by the original Creator, my grandmother created a personal memento to travel via United States mail to loved ones in another state. Over fifty years later, the same letter had been resurrected to find its way home to me. Because it had been kept for as long as the receiver could, the drawing now remains a valued piece of art for me and my family. I will cherish it always, and I too plan to keep it "for as long as" I can.

11

A Legacy, Not Copycat Creativity

by Terrie Hellard-Brown

Granny squares sat in a basket by her chair. She had just come in from working in her front yard filled with flowers and so many varied plants. She could make anything grow, it seemed. She began fixing a feast for the whole extended family, a fiesta of Mexican food and bubble bread. This was my grandmother, and she was amazing. She made us laugh even in some of the toughest times because she never let the sadness or difficulties overtake her. I learned so much from her, and she was the first to show me imagination at work.

Her daughter, my mom, followed in her mother's footsteps. She was also creative. She crocheted colorful blankets, made plants grow inside and outside our home (she called it her herbal therapy), and made the best enchiladas I've ever tasted. I think she may have even outdone Grandma's! Her favorite outlet for her ingenuity was sewing. She sewed nearly all our clothes growing up, made amazing clothes for our dolls from baby dolls to Barbies, and even tailored suits for my dad. She was creative, talented, and strong.

I'm a creative as well. However, my crocheting attempts are mangled knots of yarn looking pathetic on the floor. Most of my plants die despite my best attempts and intentions. I took sewing in school and made an apron, a bag, and a top. I passed the class, but that's about all I can say about it. My sister seems to have gotten the crocheting, botanical, and seamstress genes. My creativity sprouted in different directions than my grandma, mom, and sister. I paint. I write. I make jewelry. I sing. I hope I'm clever and talented, but I'm pretty sure I'm strong—I have a lot of good examples in my family of strong, creative women. I'm certain I was destined to be this way, and really can't help myself. If I'm not making something, I feel lost, bored, or useless. Something is always bubbling around in my mind—a story to be told or some object waiting for me to bring it into reality. I love it, and I know none of this is really anything for me to boast about. I received it from a grandmother, mother, and family who let me be the inventive misfit in my wild, creative family. And beyond that, I know all our ingenuity comes from the Creator of all things. Made in his image, he inspires us to create. He brought something from nothing, but we take what he's given us to produce something that hopefully blesses others.

I'm so thankful that my grandma, mom, and others in my family encouraged the imagination God placed in my heart and spurred me on to tell the stories growing there. They didn't expect me to be a copycat, but they celebrated the kind of ingenuity God gave me. Because of them, I am trying to pass on the legacy of creativity, strength, and encouragement. My two daughters are also not copycat creatives. My older daughter draws mythical animals and dragons while dreaming of writing a science fiction novel filled with the world and creatures she has imagined. I can't wait to read it someday.

My younger daughter is a photographer and has some of the most amazing pictures from her adventures around the world. She also creates gorgeous pen and ink art.

They both have faithfully begun to share the creativity God has placed in their hearts. My prayer is that they too will carry on the legacy of strength.

I firmly believe God has a creative story for each of us to tell. Sometimes we tell it through colors on a canvas, words on a page, or in cultivating flowers to bloom. Sometimes we live it out as a mother teaching her children to follow their Creator faithfully. Life requires creativity and strength. We come by it naturally—just look at our Father.

12

Let the Forces of Nature Declare God's Glory

by Laura Dorsey

Hear ye, hear ye, hear ye!

THE HEIRS OF THE KINGDOM OF GOD ARE MAKING

THEIR PROCLAMATIONS NOW!

WE decree

TSUNAMIS of Love over the nations,

WE decree

THUNDERSTORMS of Truth into the atmospheres,

WE decree

MONSOONS of Salvations throughout the Earth,

WE decree

LIGHTNING to strike into the hearts of men and women the

Awe of God,

WE decree

TORNADOES of God's Goodness to lead people to repentance,

WE decree

SNOWSTORMS of God's Grace to cover repented sins,

WE decree

RAINSTORMS of Peace to wash the inner soul,

WE decree

HURRICANES of Kindness to heal the broken-hearted,
WE decree
FLOODS of the Oil of Joy over those who are mourning,
WE decree
WHIRLWINDS of Mercy & Forgiveness to surround those who
have wronged us,
WE decree
VOLCANOES of Unity to erupt into the body of Christ,
WE decree
CYCLONES of Righteousness, Justice, and Praise to spring up
before all the nations through the power of his Word!

The Spirit of the Lord God is upon me,
Because the Lord has anointed and commissioned me
To bring good news to the humble and afflicted;
He has sent me to bind up [the wounds of] the brokenhearted,
To proclaim release [from confinement and condemnation] to the
[physical and spiritual] captives
And freedom to prisoners,
To proclaim the favorable year of the Lord,
And the day of vengeance and retribution of our God,
To comfort all who mourn,
To grant to those who mourn in Zion the following:
To give them a turban instead of dust
[on their heads, a sign of mourning],
The oil of joy instead of mourning,
The garment [expressive] of praise instead of a disheartened spirit.

So they will be called the trees of righteousness
[strong and magnificent, distinguished
for integrity, justice, and right standing with God],
The planting of the Lord, that He may be glorified."
(Isaiah 61:1–3 AMP)

DECLARATIONS CREATE

We will eat the fruit of our words.

For there is death and life in the power of our tongue.

CHOOSE LIFE

13

An Invitation from the Creator

by Susan Sage

Have you ever stood on top of a huge hill or mountain overlooking varying greens from trees and bushes, or put your toes at the edge of a lake or ocean, feeling the cool moistness between them?

A bursting sunset can take a person's breath away in awe as colors dance across the sky, bidding the day goodbye.

The hues and colors God blends together to make vibrant yellows and oranges, or pinks and purples on flower petals, are like nothing a phone camera can capture or an artist can copy.

If you've been touched by these or any other type of nature's beauty, the love of creativity has found its way into your soul. God showed us the importance of creativity from the opening verse of the Bible. In fact, it is the first glimpse we have of who he is, and it shows us his love of creation.

In the beginning, God created (Genesis 1:1 NKJV). Genesis chapter one uses the exact phrase, *Then God said*, in verses 6, 9, 11, 14, 20, 24, and 26 to show us how he created.

But he took it further.

***And the LORD God formed man of the dust of the ground, and breathed into his nostrils the breath of life; and man became a living being** (Genesis 2:7 **NKJV**).*

God breathed life into Adam and then gave him the job of naming all the creatures God had made.

What did Adam use to do the job God gave him? He didn't have any background or life experience to draw from. How could he have been creative enough to come up with the ideas for every name of those animals?

The simple answer: God.

The more significant answer: God never left him to do it alone.

And he doesn't leave us to do our creative work alone, either. It starts by remembering that the "our" in that sentence is not you and me, but God and each one of us individually.

Some people believe God created the world, then stepped back, and is now simply watching things happen. Is it possible some people envision their skills in this way, thinking God gave them their abilities and stepped away? With this view, a special relational part of the process is missing.

God was the most essential part of Adam's naming of the animals. In the same way, it's important for him to be involved in crafting sentences, mixing paint colors, spinning clay on a wheel, sketching a figure, or coming up with a new recipe. Without his influence, how well are we representing him to those who will enjoy the fruit of our efforts?

Often, writers talk about inviting God into their writing time, which sounds like a good plan. Perhaps artists ask God to bless what goes from the brush to the canvas. Maybe a knitter seeks God's favor on their hands for the outcome.

But what if we flipped things? If all ideas come from him and all artistry flows from his creativity, perhaps it is he who is inviting us.

How would that thought change how we view what we are doing?

At times, we can get caught up in a performance-based mentality. I've wasted too much energy and time trying to prove myself in different ways. But when the applause of others is my focus, all I end up with is disappointment and frustration. Maybe you've experienced the same thing.

A shift of perspective could adjust that and keep us from striving, allowing us to thrive in the gift of creativity God gave us. This would also mean we are not focused on outcome-based work but rather on faithfulness to what God has breathed into us.

When I take the time to sit with God before beginning anything, peace settles deep inside, my heart beats a bit slower, and I am not as easily distracted. When I acknowledge that the project I'm working on is God's and that he has given it to me to do, I don't worry so much about how many likes, comments, or responses I receive. The work is his, as is the result.

God's word says,

For we are his workmanship, created in Christ Jesus for good works, which God prepared ahead of time for us to do.
(Ephesians 2:10 CSB)

God invites us into the work and the world of creativity designed for us before time began.

This invitation reminds us that from Him [*all things originate*] and through Him [*all things live and exist*] and to Him are all things [*directed*].

To Him be glory and honor forever (Romans 11:36 AMP)!

Imagine seeing the wonder of our creativity in the same way we take in the mountaintop view or feel the refreshing touch of toes in cool water. As we acknowledge God and step into his invitation to create with him, a new appreciation could capture our hearts, like the colors of a sunset or flowers. This invitation to engage on this level with God, instead of him stepping into our world, could breathe new life and give us a fresh spark on laborious days when we're polishing or reworking whatever we've created.

Be encouraged to take a step of faith into the beautiful world of creativity, and become a part of God's continuing work at his invitation.

14

Recalibration

by Christopher Myers

This is a time for you to recalibrate and enjoy what I'm doing, God said as I prepared to move from my home of twelve years with no sure destination. Spend the next three months relaxing and focusing on me. Watch what I do.

At first I considered the recalibration necessary to finally rid myself of lingering scars and unpleasant attitudes that surfaced now and again—results of running a design-build company in New York City for sixteen years. It had been an awful experience, and I didn't just drink a little and have sex infrequently. My misery kept me tethered to my sins, and I grew to hate myself rather than my sins.

A persistent self-hatred fueled my choice to do things I disliked. I wasn't secretly trying to avoid work; I chose hard work over what I avoided—to serve the kingdom as a writer. No way would God want me to be a kingdom servant. I felt unworthy.

***But he is faithful, and God's gifts and his call are irrevocable** (Romans 11:29 NIV).*

While still running the company, God's Spirit mercifully inspired me to find my house in Summer Haven, Florida. During my first year there, God's Spirit extracted me from my selfish perspectives by replacing them with joyful experiences he'd curated without my help. I traveled each month throughout Florida and discovered well-being when I allowed the Spirit to lead. I began a memoir, *The Sound of Palms*, which chronicled the journeys in a self-help-style travelogue. Despite the anguish during this transitional time, I took hold of God's hand.

On the beach, after I'd read the first draft of *The Sound of Palms* and in disgust said, "I'm a terrible writer," God was there to encourage and love me.

This is why I brought you to this place, this beach. Here is where you'll learn to write, God whispered.

This intimate divine insight encouraged me to continue to write, and month after month, I slowly found my way back into his good, pleasing, and perfect will (Romans 12:2 NIV). It felt great to be in Florida, exploring and writing, and opening my heart to the Lord. He was revealing my true nature, the real me.

It took ten years of rehabilitation on long beach walks to open my heart to understand that the toxins of willful sin and doing what I didn't believe in had kept me blind to the pleasure of pursuing what I loved, the call, the passion he put in me.

The time came to trust God and close the company. He brought circumstances that allowed me to segue into writing full-time: I sold my house and rented it back for two years. I entered a new season of creativity.

I grew as a writer, stories were published, and I completed *The Sound of Palms*. My love and understanding of my island community of marshes and coastline deepened as I painted and exhibited my paintings. The more I painted the beautiful horizon of sea and sky, the more I wanted to explore the thin line between heaven and earth. It wasn't about my creativity; it was about my Creator. I felt stirred to know him closer than ever before. I felt his abundant love taking over where judgment had ruled. My creativity began to transform into an authentic peaceful expression of my being, rather than the results-driven process I had known most of my life.

My creativity sought out theological wonder, and my heart began a quest to understand this way of life so I could confidently hit the restart button. A door opened to earn my Master of Arts in Practical Theology. Having the time and provision felt like a practical miracle. I realized that where I lived—and my circumstances—were my treasure. And in my treasure, God was present and desirous to engage with me. This became the topic for my thesis: Discovering Your Treasure: How God Uses Place and Circumstance to Engage with His People.

Before the two-year rent-back period ended, I'd searched for new places to live, applied for jobs, and prayed fervently for guidance. Despite my efforts, God revealed his way forward—recalibration. My spirit wasn't freaked out or full of anxiety. God's peace in me brought deeper understanding: I expected his provision rather than relying on my strength.

One definition of recalibration, according to Merriam-Webster, is to calibrate again; adjust precisely for a particular function. This made sense. Over time, I'd grown to trust my skills and experiences instead of maintaining a robust trust in God and his ways. When a compass gets knocked about, the calibration needs tweaking. Like the compass, I needed a trusted expert to perform a recalibration. My focus became, *Trust in the Lord with all your heart* (Proverbs 3:5 NIV).

I had no idea how much help I needed packing. But God knew! He inspired a dear friend, LB, to offer her generous assistance. "I'm a great packer. It's a gift of mine. I'll give you as much help as you need."

I accepted her help.

During that week of boxes, tape, towels, blankets, pots, pans, bric-a-brac, books, and fabulous cocktails and meals, LB offered her vacant house on St. Simons Island, Georgia, to me and my yellow Labrador, Honey. I smiled in acknowledgment but shrugged it off as too good to be true.

The next day I packed up my paints and felt awash with the satisfaction of how God does things. I pondered biking and walking on the beach on St. Simons Island.

Is LB's house my next stop? I asked God, with the assurance that he was for me and my good. In my heart, I felt the reassurance of peace. I accepted her offer.

A week later my mother visited to help. I relinquished former preconceptions and accepted her love for me without anxious expectations. I marveled at God's suggestion to give my mother boxes of memorabilia to sort, and my spirit delighted with calm joy as I watched her work.

"Do you want this anymore?" she asked, holding a windup bull from the Plaza del Sol I'd purchased on a high school class trip in Madrid.

My reaction was to hold onto everything that had a positive memory, but I said, "No, it's time to let that go."

It felt good to let go of expectations and things I had held onto. With less than a week left, I had to let go of my home as well.

I walked Honey up to the beach where we swam and lay flat

on the sandy expanse to dry off. I looked up at the deep blue sky, listened to the waves, and began to cry. "Lord, you've been so good to me here. Thank you."

LB and her husband, Brett, returned to help me pack the moving truck. To lighten our load, a handyman friend gifted a day of his services to help lift and schlepp the heavy stuff. I felt looked after in a way that went beyond what money for creative abilities could provide. God's Spirit revealed a new territory in my spirit: a place where I could stop using creativity as a commodity, stop hating myself, and finally accept my value in terms of love and acceptance. I received the love that others were genuinely offering. It was relational manna.

Wave after wave of unconditional love flows through as I settle into the house on St. Simons Island. A noisy downpour refreshes.

Taking a break on the screened porch, I'm learning that not being hard on myself allows more intimacy with God's Spirit. I savor the breezes and enjoy the beauty of ancient oak trees dripping with rain and moss.

I'm mesmerized by the sound of rain on leaves, roofs, and downspouts out here under gray skies. I realize I was taught creativity by teachers outside God's kingdom who instilled a ruthless quality in their lessons: Creativity must pay your bills; if not, you're a failure. The rain tapers off and pedestrians and revelers in golf carts go by the house in the spirit of vacation and leisure. As I watch them with Honey at my feet, I feel a weight lift. I see the misguided notion that I've attached my value to my work and the approval of others. My spirit overflows with relief.

My value is unearned. It's from you and you call me yours. How marvelous you would bring me to this place to impart my true value, filling my spirit, soul, and being. This is a holy recalibration. I'm reminded of a favorite verse:

***Do not conform any longer to the pattern of this world, but be transformed by the renewing of your mind. Then you will be able to test and approve what God's will is—his good, pleasing, and perfect will* (Romans 12:2 NIV).**

Thank you, Lord. Lead on.

15

We Praise You, Our Creator

by Terrie Hellard-Brown

I see the intricacies of your creative work

In the baby's sleepy smile,

In the spirals of a seashell,

In the wild sunset colors,

In the majesty of snow-capped mountains,

In the zoomies of my dog.

I feel the genius of your creative power

In the waves moving sand under my feet,

In the strong winds blowing raindrops sideways,

In the icy fluff of snowdrifts freezing my toes,

In the vibrations of thunderclaps before the rain begins,

In the relieving coolness of evening after a scorching day.

I hear the blessing of your diverse gifts

In the morning song of the birds by my window,

In the terrifying roar of giant Asian lions at the Singapore Zoo,

In the laughter of children, no matter where we are in the world,

In the deep notes of a baritone singing praises to You,

In the words of love expressed between family.

I taste the extravagance of your creative provision

In the sweet, drippy bite into a mango,

In the sharp tartness of a pomegranate,

In the savory satisfaction of salted, buttery vegetables,

In the pure sweetness of honey,

In the sour pucker from lemon.

I smell your unbelievable attention to detail

In the evening bloom of jasmine,

In the nostalgia of cinnamon and apples in autumn,

In the soft sweetness of a spring breeze,

In the joy of a newborn's scent,

In the familiar fragrance of home.

You created for us

Your heart inspires us to create and bless—to think of others.

Your creativity inspires

Awe

Worship

Gratitude.

Thank you for creating so many blessings for us to enjoy.

We praise you, our Creator.

16

The Blue Bird of Happiness

by Debbie Jones Warren

Pushing her cat-eye glasses further up her slender nose, my fourth grade teacher bends over my desk. "Debbie, it looks like you're still having trouble counting American money."

I frown and point to number four on my workbook page with black marks and smudges all over. "I'll never figure this out. Did I get this one right, yet?" In our missionary boarding school in Nigeria, I get confused by American math.

The teacher shakes her head, and her floral perfume floats through the air. "No. A quarter plus a nickel makes thirty cents, not thirty-five cents."

I tug at my hair, my frustration mounting. "I can never remember how much a quarter, a dime, and a nickel are worth." I look up at her frowning face and grin. "But I know how many Nigerian shillings are in a pound."

The teacher sighs and stands tall. "The rest of the students completed this section last week. You should have it memorized by now."

"Isn't a nickel worth ten cents? It's bigger than a dime, so the dime should be five cents. It doesn't make any sense to me." Then I giggle. "I made a joke. Sense sounds the same as cents!"

She turns and strides toward the front of the classroom, her heels clicking on the cement floor. I think she's mad at me.

When she reaches her desk, she says, "Class, it's time to put away your arithmetic books and take out your geography textbooks."

Oh, goody. I love geography. It's always a bright spot in my day. I love looking at the world maps and dreaming of where my parents are, four hundred miles south on their mission station.

The teacher clears her throat. "Please open to Chapter Eight."

On the first page of the chapter, there's a picture of an island with a white sandy beach lined with shady palm trees. Beautiful blue-green ocean waves lap at the shore. I'd like to sail away and live there.

As we take turns reading the paragraphs, my mind drifts away to the island in the Pacific Ocean where little, brown-skinned boys shimmy up palm trees and harvest coconuts. Smiling little girls dance with straw skirts twirling, and birds call loudly to each other in the trees.

When the bell rings, I startle and pull myself back from my daydream.

Our teacher shuts her book. "Class is dismissed." She walks to the side wall and stops in front of the Progress Chart. Down the left-hand side of the poster, all our names are listed in a column. To the right of each name is a paper race car. Across the top, numbers show each of the sections in arithmetic. All the cars have progressed halfway across the poster. Except mine, which lags.

The teacher speaks once more, "Good work, class. Debbie, you're the only one who didn't complete today's section. You need to work harder."

One by one, she moves each car ahead to the next column. But the car on my line stays in place way behind the others. My shoulders slump, and I shuffle out the door.

The next morning, I skip across the playground from the dorm to the school building. Already the bright African sun has warmed the monkey bars, and I do a quick flip while holding my dress tucked between my knees. I hope we do something fun in class today.

After we finally finish the boring math lesson, the teacher makes an announcement. "Today we have arts and crafts."

Yippee! I like that even better than geography.

The teacher explains the project. "Each of you will make a decorative item to give someone in your family for Christmas."

As she walks to the back of the room, her yellow skirt swishes around her knees. "I'll give everyone some plaster of Paris, and you'll press it into a mold of your choosing."

On the big table in the back of the classroom sit two dozen plastic molds with shapes of trees, cars, flowers, and animals. I scan the choices, then grab a mold of a little bird sitting on a branch.

I turn to the girl next to me. "Doesn't this bird look so sweet? It's plain now, but I know my mom will think it's beautiful after I paint it."

She smiles. "Yes. And I love this bouquet of flowers I'm making for my mom. Don't you?"

I nod. We return to our desks and get to work. The plaster is cool in my hands, and soon our desks are a white mess.

The teacher helps me press a small safety pin into the back of my project. "You've done a nice job on this, Debbie. Your mom is an artist, and once you paint it, I know she'll be pleased." She pats me on the back. "The pin sticks out so the bird can be worn on her dress as a brooch."

Then she turns to the middle of the room. "In a few days, your projects will dry, and you'll paint them. When you fly home at Christmas, you can take your projects with you."

Friday is the big day. The plaster for my craft project is dry. I tug my little bird out of the mold, choose my paints, and begin to work at my seat. I paint the body blue, then add orange for the feet and yellow for the beak. Mom loves the birds that sing outside our mission house on the edge of the rainforest in southern Nigeria.

I miss my mom so much when I'm here at school. I'm glad to have something to give her for Christmas.

During my first four years at Kent Academy (KA), I really struggled. I didn't do well with academics or obeying the rules in the dorm or eating the food in the dining room. Living away from home at such a young age without the guidance and nurture of my parents took a toll.

In my early years, navigating all the rules and social interactions was so traumatic I couldn't focus on classwork. Later, in junior high and high school, I got As and Bs. Making this little blue bird was a joyful, creative venture. It was one of the few times I had the opportunity to create something beautiful with my hands. Giving it as a gift to my mom gave me even more joy than creating it for myself.

Sometimes I have wondered if my childhood memories really happened. That's when I go to our KA Facebook group and check to see what things other adult KA kids remember. I've never asked about this craft day, even though I've often thought about the precious blue bird the teacher helped me make.

Today I live on another continent and in a different culture. In all the moves from boarding school to home, from Nigeria to California, I lost things. My childhood was disjointed, fragmented. My parents missed out on many aspects of my life at school, and not all of my craft projects made it home.

Last June I helped my mom, who is ninety-one, move to Assisted Living from an independent retirement home. The sixteen years she'd spent there were the longest time she'd lived in one place. As we sorted through her accumulated belongings, she bemoaned the fact she'd kept so much clutter.

I celebrated it. Throughout the weeks, I uncovered many treasured mementos representing our family's history: household guest books from our years in Nigeria chronicling the people we hosted; curios and artifacts created by Nigerian craftsmen; the last pieces of her renowned salt and pepper shaker collection.

Lifting the lid off a small cardboard box, I pushed aside a yellowed square of cotton. My eyes opened wide as this little bird flew into my hands. It found me, all these years later, telling me how much I was treasured by my mother.

She'd kept the plaster of Paris gift I made for her years ago in fourth grade. I was relieved to know my childhood memories created in a far-off land were real after all. Mom was an artist, but I didn't think I'd inherited the artistic gene. Sure enough, the paint job was splotchy, looking very much like a clumsy nine-year-old had painted it. However, this precious brooch reminded me that created items don't have to be perfect in order to be valued.

Finding this treasured item from my childhood reassured me of God's enduring love. His thoughts are always for me, and I'm the apple of his eye. He is our Creator. We're made in his image, and each of us has a little bit of a creative spark inside. When we ignite the spark, it brings joy to us and to our loving Father.

17

Explosive Creativity

by Lainey La Shay

I t all starts with a spark. A breath so small no one notices. A glow deep in the core that begins to grow. It gains strength, expanding until it flashes into heat. Everything around it goes molten, stirred into wild currents. It strives to find its way to the surface, to find expression, to burst into endless varieties of color and dimension. To become marvelous creation.

Do you have the courage to seek it? Or are you hesitant to set your boots on my slopes? Come navigate the twists and turns—the deep crevasses and braided heights—that lead to my summit. There you will discover a roaring fountain spewing red-hot creativity into the starry sky. Creativity dances here like liquid fire, igniting everything it touches, and overflowing in a riot of color as it cascades into new spaces.

The rivers of creation solidify into new landscapes, removing the old and building new foundations on which to grow. This fertile land allows endless possibilities to bloom. The recharging of the atmosphere gives new breath and inspiration to the world. The most powerful force on Earth has the ability to destroy—or bring abundant life. Yet there are people so frightened of creativity that they seek to douse the outpouring of fiery creation in any way they can. They perceive it as a dangerous threat that needs to be stopped. For a time, they may even appear successful as they quell it in even the most creative of people. However, creativity cannot be stifled. It will burst from the seams and explode from the depths, and those who try to stop it will be subducted under the passion of its ravenous rivers.

Are you trembling? Why do you fear stepping into the unknown—to climb the peak and witness the raw energy of creation? Is it the fear of being scalded by the rush of heat running up to greet you? Or will taking this adventure vaporize your fragile sense of safety and control?

Do you treat creativity like a volcano—as something of which to be afraid? A stunning mountain to have in your landscape as long as she's quiet and calm? If so, you misunderstand her. She is a creation of the Most High God—a creation intended to create. A creation intended to worship.

She sings with joy to dance before her creator because he perfectly placed every stone and ignited the fire in her heart. She melts like wax in her sculptor's hands. How much more does he want to flood you with the pure fire of his creative spirit to bring vibrant life and change into the world around you? As with the volcanic wild, he designed you to flourish with creativity. Let the rumblings in your heart grow. Let them echo through the crevasses and hollows of your soul and begin to build something new. Follow the calling he has given you. Feel the creativity burst in a fountain of light from you and explore the directions in which it wants to flow. Let it melt away your inhibitions and self-imposed barriers. Experience the joy of worship through creation.

And let it begin with a spark.

18

Making the Most of It

by Christine Hagion

Since childhood I've always been a gift-giver. From fresh-picked flowers to sloppy mud pies, I always presented my offerings with a wide grin.

The Lord blessed me with a rich imagination. As an adult this enables me to be resourceful and design things that cause others to marvel. He also placed within me a creative spirit, giving joy to me and others.

Yet there was a period in my life, decades ago, which vanquished all hope. My creative muse was comatose.

Three weeks before Christmas, I boarded a Greyhound bus at dawn carrying only a diaper bag, my newborn, and my Bible. Fleeing Los Angeles, where my ex-husband was searching for me, I settled down into the cushioned seat while holding my infant in my lap. It's going to be a long ride to Northern California. Please God, let her remain quiet and not upset the other riders, I prayed silently.

As the bus left the station and traversed the menacing streets, I could imagine my abuser lurking behind any one of the buildings. He'd been stalking me for months.

"Your husband keeps calling, looking for you," the receptionist at my obstetrician's office had reported at an earlier prenatal appointment. I'd taken refuge in a battered women's shelter. Was he still looking for me? It was a risk I was unwilling to take.

What would my life look like now, several hundreds of miles away? I had no idea. Safety was my only concern—for me and my little one, whom he'd tried to kill while she was yet inside me. We'd escaped with our lives and nothing else. Except my faith.

My older sister was aware of my dilemma, offering to let me stay a while with her family. I only hoped that I'd not put them in danger as well.

Along the way I spoke with the older fellow sitting next to me who shared that he had just been released from prison for manslaughter. He recounted punching someone in the throat during a drunken brawl, and lamented spending two decades behind bars for one stupid split-second decision. I remarked that we were both fleeing a hellish existence to a new, unknown life. He smiled, perhaps surprised to have been met with compassion instead of judgment.

The bus pulled into the station and I waved goodbye, wishing him well before disembarking. I glimpsed my sister's familiar face among the crowd assembling to pick up passengers.

"Hey, Crust," Heidi greeted me with her favorite teenage nickname. She'd loved calling me "Crustacean," mangling my name into a moniker.

"Hey, Heidelbaum," I shot back, cracking a smile. My strawberry-blonde hair got caught underneath straps as I slung the diaper bag onto my shoulder. Our embrace was warm but awkward with the newborn in my arms.

While driving to her home, Heidi told me about her best

friend living next door, and how their kids played together. I hope I'm not imposing too much on their lives. Finally, we turned onto a large field.

"We're home," she announced.

This unpaved road is her driveway? I saw only agricultural fields.

"Where's your house?"

"That's it, right there," she replied, pointing to a long, arched hut in the dirt made from corrugated steel. It looked like a structure where farm workers packed fruit before sending it to market. Why was she living here? I scratched my head and followed her.

"Mommy!" Her two small children chanted in unison as Heidi opened the door. They ran to her, hugging her legs.

"Hold on. Let me get inside already!" She pointed to me. "Do you remember your aunt, Christy?"

They nodded, then ran over and squeezed me, their cherubic faces looking up at mine.

Heidi had moved the girls' twin bed into the living room for me; they'd sleep in their parents' bed. We fashioned a small makeshift room by hanging string from one wall to another, draping a bedsheet across for privacy.

That night I walked toward the bathroom in the dark.

Eeeek! I heard the shriek of an animal in pain.

Flicking on the light, I discovered a long tail underneath my foot. I yelped and jumped, watching in horror as hundreds of little brown mice scurried across the linoleum to hide in the kitchen cupboards. I tried to steady my breathing and calm my thoughts.

In their extreme poverty, they took me in. I will be grateful despite the conditions. A Scripture popped into my mind:

***Better a dry crust eaten with peace and quiet than a house full of feasting, with strife* (Proverbs17:1 NIV).**

Even living in the dirt with mice was better than being beaten by someone who vowed to love me.

The following day Heidi pulled out her artificial Christmas tree, and we all joined in the decorating. Her two daughters played dress-up, wrapping the garland around their necks and shoulders like a feather boa. Eventually the gold fuzzy strand got placed on their tree, and we sipped cocoa, sitting back to admire our handiwork.

In this otherwise-joyful moment, my thoughts turned to her small children, imagining their disappointment when there was no gift from their auntie for them under the tree. I'd spent what little money I had on the bus ticket. I only have pennies in my pocket. I cannot buy them anything. What can I do?

I shared my dilemma with Heidi, who then led me into her bedroom. Among her few things was a box containing scraps of material.

"You're welcome to anything in there," she told me, pointing. "You're imaginative. Maybe you can make them something."

Rummaging through it, I found bits of ribbon, a few random buttons and snaps, smallish pieces of fabric. What on earth can I make with this?

Just then, Heather, my two-year-old niece, ran into the bedroom, wearing a pink construction paper crown atop her little head. Heidi's children were young enough to still inhabit the fairy-tale world of princesses and castles and kings on horses. Suddenly, an idea popped into my mind.

I asked whether Heidi had an old unwanted pole. After scrounging around in a closet, she found a broom with broken bristles, handing it to me. This would be perfect! My creative juices were flowing.

Breaking off the brush, I asked her husband to saw the handle in two when he returned home from work. Having no sandpaper, I rasped both pieces over rough concrete outside, smoothing the cut edges. After ensuring the girls would not get splinters in their little fingers, I moved on to the next phase of my project.

I requested that Heidi keep the little ones out of her bedroom while Santa's red-haired elf was hard at work in the makeshift workshop. On the back of a paper grocery bag, I drew an outline of an animal head. Cutting one thickness of the underside of chalky blue fabric around the template, I turned it over for an opposite image and traced again before snipping it with scissors. I repeated this with a dingy green material I hoped to dress up afterward.

The sewing box accompanied me everywhere for a few days. In between breastfeeding my baby and helping Heidi with household chores, I sewed the fabric pieces by hand. Inverting them once the seams were strong enough, I stuffed them loosely with tufts of fiberfill from an old torn pillow. They were beginning to take shape, and I could feel my excitement rise.

Thrilled when I found two different pairs of matching buttons, I sewed a black set onto the blue fabric, and chose brown ones for the green material, to make matching button eyes. I added more white fluff to both heads until they were firmly packed. I attached ribbon onto each, and embroidered pink tongues. Inserting dowels into the two stuffed pieces, I poured white glue generously, and placed them upside-down, supported by books on both sides to dry.

On Christmas morning the girls ran to the Christmas tree, eager to see what Santa had brought. Heather squealed when she unwrapped a baby doll. Jessica beamed at her plastic shopping cart with pretend food in vegetable shapes. Then came the moment of truth: Would they appreciate my meager offering?

I'd had nothing appropriate for wrapping the gifts: their impractical, odd shapes only fit in large black garbage bags with bows. Jessica opened hers first, revealing a blue stick horse with a bridle made of red ribbon, and brown yarn for the mane. The green one was Heather's, with a yellow-ribboned bridle and rust-colored mane. They shouted joyfully at their homemade gifts, immediately mounting them, and pretended to gallop throughout the realm of their Quonset Hut kingdom.

Tapping into creativity helped me reclaim joy amidst my trauma. In one conversation Moses had with God, the Lord asked, *What is that in your hand?* (Exodus 4:2 ESV). For Moses, it was a rod. For me, it was a box of scraps.

19

Out of Nothing

by Joyce D. Hightower

What did God think when considering the nothingness of Earth? It stood without recognizable value, consequence, or significance, and had no form or structure.

If you or I see something unknown, our logical minds search through every item we have experienced. The goal is to make a connection and identify something we've encountered before. Our memories proudly declare it is similar to one of those things, although not precisely the same.

For God, this was no haphazard discovery or accidental mutation. He was not out looking for a suitable place to inscribe his name, for it was written on every single thing. It was not out of ambition, for he is the almighty God. When he surveyed the earth, it was out of a profound love. He desired to provide a good place for his children, human beings. They were to be like nothing else. Made in his image, they could envelop his Spirit, reflect aspects of his nature, and be in a relationship with him. Where would he place them?

This was not just a planet's creation but a cosmic stage's setting. God brought something new from chaos and darkness with his words' power. He orchestrated the order and timing of history's unfolding, and balanced the galaxy of innumerable stars in the heavens. One star at the center of a solar system brought a schedule to govern the passage of time on planet Earth. Firm ground separated from the waters, and a garden was placed in the center of that ground. There, the most amazing delights for enjoyment grew and flourished. Everything made up to this point was pronounced good and told to produce after its kind.

The time came for the special limited edition to be made. This was not a being to be spoken into existence like all the others. This being was designed and formed by God's own hands. He then received God's breath of life and became a unique tripartite reflection of God himself, the Trinity. Adam awoke in the quiet garden as a living soul, a spiritual and emotional mixture with the freedom to make spiritual choices and relate to God. At the same time, he could feel love, peace, hate, and anger. He awoke with a physical body, allowing him to function in the physical environment and enjoy delicate fragrances, beautiful sunrise skies, melodies of the tiny birds in the trees above, and taste the sweet, succulent fruit growing all around. He was equipped with wisdom and intellect to not only name all of the rest of creation, but also care for it.

Just as God desired a relationship with Adam, his imprinted creation, a part of Adam also wanted a relationship with someone like him. Eve was formed. And in perfect peace and joy, they lived in the garden, the ideal place with all they needed. It might have seemed like this should have gone on for ages. But earth was a battleground, and there were always losses in war.

God included blood red and betrayal yellow in his creation palette. At the very beginning, he had been sure to provide for the leather to be used for the whip that tore into the back of Jesus, the tree to provide wood for the crucifixion cross, and the rocks to be hewn for a short stay in the grave. Nothing was left out.

Creation was not an attempt, a good try, or a well-done act. It was a perfect effort. The war was won. We walk, work, breathe, think, and invent today because, from the beginning, God's love covered every detail. The silence of the original nothing, Earth, reverberates with joy. That's the sound of rejoicing on Earth and in Heaven with the salvation of a new child of God.

From what had once been nothing came a kingdom of truth believers. The number of those in the kingdom was more than anyone could count. Incredible. That is creativity at a God level.

20

God's Creativity

by Adrienne N. Wartts

We've all had a tough time finding a solution to a problem, right? Maybe for you it was a career-related hurdle, a marital problem, an issue with your child at school, or a health crisis. I know I have faced challenges that were not possible for me to resolve in my own strength.

But I know I can do all things through Christ who strengthens me (Philippians 4:13 NJKV).

So, I pray. And when I enter into a collaborative effort in which I follow God's lead, he creates solutions. Let me share two examples of how he has responded to obstacles.

For a milestone birthday gift, I wanted to purchase my own home. One year beforehand, I began looking for homes and located the property I wanted. The home was in a charming neighborhood near my job. However, I didn't earn enough money to qualify for a home loan or even make a down payment. Although my dream felt far-fetched, I prayed about it. I did not hear anything from God, but he obviously kept my desire in mind. Without me realizing it, he was working behind the scenes and creating all the right circumstances. Within months God blessed me with a merit increase, a cost-of-living increase, and a promotional increase. My salary doubled in less than one year. I did not have to work harder or seek a higher-paying job. A few months before my birthday, I noticed the home I wanted was still on the market. God took my problem and created provision. Two weeks before my birthday, I moved into my dream home.

Another challenge occurred when my career drifted me more than 1,000 miles away from my family in the Midwest. When the 2020 pandemic occurred, I resided in New England. For many people, the two-year plague resulted in great loss, such as the loss of freedom to travel and roam, loss of loved ones, and loss of employment. Perhaps we were all negatively impacted in one way or another. But while the pandemic appeared to spiral further and further out of control, a major shift started occurring in my life. I noticed God unraveling ways for me to become acquainted with work-life balance.

It started with the new remote-work model, which eventually led me back to the Midwest and reunited me with my loved ones. Plus, not having to rush into an office any more allowed me to sleep a little longer each morning. I saved money I used to spend on food purchases at work as an alternative to making breakfast, coffee, and lunch at home. I gained more minutes at the end of my work day given that I no longer had to sit in rush-hour traffic. And I saved on gas and mileage. The shift personally felt like God's way of creating an opportunity to supply me with abundance. He blessed me with more time with my family, ample rest, healthier food choices, and more money in my savings account. Now, if that is not the epitome of God's creativity, then what else can I tell you?

I hope I have inspired you to reflect on how God has manifested your dreams and provided you with solutions.

There are many things we simply cannot accomplish on our own, but with God, all things are possible.
(Matthew 19:26 NIV)

So, if you haven't already, I encourage you to ask him to intercede in your life. Remember to ask him in the name of Jesus. Then, watch how he creates opportunities for you to flourish in your career. See how he leads you closer to your loved ones. Marvel at how he pivots you into a new way of approaching many of the complex situations we all encounter as we journey through this earthly experience known as life.

21

God's Strength in Creation

by Dian L. Avila

Waves ripple, swell, tower, break, and shine in a multitude of hues in everything from rain puddles to vast oceans—each crest demonstrating God's beauty and might. A puddle can grow to flood a city and waves can topple the largest ships, but God is in control of each drop.

> ***Mightier than the thunder of the great waters, mightier than the breakers of the sea—the Lord on high is mighty.***
> **(Psalm 93:4 NIV)**

My daughter, Candace, introduced twenty-month-old Matea to the sea with the water washing over her at waist level. Mom bobbed with her little one in water as calm as a pond. They turned to wave at me on the beach, but disappeared under a big swell that snatched Matea out of Candace's arms. I jumped up knowing I was too far away to help. Candace latched onto one of Matea's arms and brought her back, lifting her up out of the water, wide-eyed and coughing. Praise God Candace wasn't knocked off her feet and still had one hand on Matea. This is a picture of what God does as he protects us from the great waters because He is mightier!

When one of life's storms erupts, our tendency is to wonder how long we will have to suffer. The answer is always out there past the shores we long to land on. Sometimes we secretly find islands to wade onto and pretend the storm has passed, getting sucked into binge watching, hiding in our homes or spending the days scrolling on our phones. Those who veer into even darker waters for relief only find fiercer squalls. We all have been in the same storm of life in a broken world on different currents, in different vessels. And God, our best friend, Adonai, is in each boat and is with us in all our struggles.

I will be with you; and when you pass through the rivers, they will not sweep over you (Isaiah 43:2 NIV).

Truly we can only rest on quiet waters in certain seasons, but the true shore and eternal rest is when we reach heaven and live with our Lord for eternity. We can see a reflection of heaven and its beauty in everything God created.

God led my husband, Jose, and I to move to Peru as missionaries in 2000, along with our three children. We flew from Lima through the Andes, past towering mountains, through puffy clouds, and over the Amazon jungle. Trees as far as you could see in a 180 degree panorama spread below us. Gray ribbons wound through the sea of trees. I'd had a desire to see the rainforest since I was in fifth grade, and now I was going to live there.

We took a small Cessna plane to the remote jungle where our future teammates were living in thatched roofed houses on the banks of the Purus River. I was soaking in the whole experience, the tapestry of green, the spider monkey and scarlet macaw they called pets. Hammocks swung inside the homes, and the sun melted into the river like a wafer into hot cocoa every evening.

A boat ride revealed pink river dolphins. Not too far from the bank was a strong current that we could swim against and stay in one place like a treadmill. Our daughter, Candace, then twelve, enjoyed this new exercise with me.

In the middle of the night, the swim Candace and I had in the river hit her. She threw off her sheet and ran out of the hut. I began pulling on my boots, grabbed a flashlight and machete, and followed her. The saying, "Those with dysentery aren't afraid of the dark," rang true for her that night. Some of you may be wondering why I grabbed a machete, the large sword-like blade used for chopping back brush, and sometimes as a weapon. I don't think I could have used it against any large threat, but it works well against isula, or bullet ants, that like to come out at night, and have the sting of a scorpion. You don't want to meet one of those in the outhouse without protection. The second time I had to run after her I was sure I heard a growl not far from behind the outhouse. The third time, I sent Jose with her and, finally, the fourth time, the sun began to rise, and she was on her own. In God's great blessing, she was all better by the time the plane came to pick us up. The natives who lived in the community confirmed there were panther tracks behind the outhouse. Praise our Lord I only heard and didn't see it. This was only the beginning of our "passing through the rivers."

When the consequence of swimming in the Purus hit me, I was not as fortunate to recover before it caused severe dehydration. I began vomiting, and could not even drink water without it coming back up. Jose had stayed in the jungle for a few more days while I acquainted myself with the town of Pucallpa. I did not realize the hospital was on the agenda. After getting the kids settled for the night, I began spending a very difficult night trying to massage out cramps in a multitude of muscles. The worst were my feet and hands. At one point I was in the entryway pacing to work out the cramps in my feet and legs and I heard singing from the nearby church. I wondered why they were gathered on a Friday and realized it was Good Friday. The church was celebrating the death of our Lord-—the night his hands and feet were nailed to a cross. I felt humbled and honored to feel pain like his on the very night we celebrate his great sacrifice. I was learning to rejoice in my suffering. I spent the night praising our Lord.

The next morning, we called a doctor, and I was admitted to the hospital for much needed intravenous fluids. Being in a hospital in a developing country was one of my biggest concerns. Well, God knew that, and I guess he figured he would take care of that concern right away. So again, the tears of joy and praise flowed as I realized God's protection and provision and his care for my heart. In the four and a half years we lived there, I was never hospitalized again.

These are just a couple of examples of how God has showed his faithfulness and grown my heart towards him. It is God's faithfulness and the way he answers prayers and gives us what we need (not always what we want) that increases our faith when we let him. When we ponder his promises and character and creation, we are inspired to be creative in the ways we praise him and live like him.

A scripture passage ties the previous two together beautifully. Try to picture being in the boat described in Matthew 8:23–27.

We know how it ends, but might read it as if we don't. Feel the suspense and terror the disciples, trained sailors, were feeling. This must have been quite a storm!

Then he got into the boat and his disciples followed him. Suddenly a furious storm came up on the lake, so that the waves swept over the boat. But Jesus was sleeping. The disciples went and woke him, saying, "Lord, save us! We're going to drown!" He replied, "You of little faith, why are you so afraid?" Then he got up and rebuked the winds and the waves, and it was completely calm. The men were amazed and asked, "What kind of man is this? Even the winds and the waves obey him!" **(Matthew 8:23–27 NIV).**

This is our God! Even the winds and waves obey him. If you have never trusted Jesus as your Lord and Savior, what are you waiting for? He loves you deeply, eternally. He longs to have you embrace his love. As Jesus said, "Why are you so afraid?"

If you've been walking with the Lord for years, but you still complain, worry, doubt—stop. Embrace his love for you. Read his word. Ponder his love for you. Replace any negative thoughts with the truth of who he is. Rejoice in all he has for you. This is a little of my experience with Jesus. He truly is love, peace, and joy for everyone!

22

The Gift of Creativity

by Terese Belme

How does it make you feel when you describe yourself as a creative? Perhaps a more direct question is: Do you believe others to be more creative than you? I used to feel this way. Sure, I can string words together, and many times these words flow together in a beautiful harmony, holding hands as if they are best friends, and dancing along on the page. However, I didn't always believe this that ability, this gift from God, gave me the authenticity to call myself creative. As I write these words, it is not lost on me—the taunt of the enemy that comes clearly into focus, and his lie that I believed for far too long.

In the beginning God (Elohim) *created* [by forming from nothing] *the heavens and the earth* (Genesis 1:1 AMP).

God created.

For in Him all things were created, things in heaven and on earth, visible and invisible, whether thrones or dominions or rulers or authorities. All things were created through Him and for Him (Colossians 1:16 BSB).

Not only did God create, but he also created all things in heaven and on earth. This reminds me that creativity is woven into our spiritual DNA.

In the past, when I've thought about creativity, I would think about those who create with crafts. I think of one friend who has the most beautiful accent and, when she pronounces the word craft, it translates as croft. She can look at a project and instantly know how much tulle and raffia are needed. She can turn a sanctuary into a Winter Wonderland during Christmas, causing you to feel you've just arrived via The Polar Express. Me? Praise God for the prefab mission kits my kids used for their fourth-grade history projects!

Several years ago, I was part of a small group that my pastor had taken to a Poets and Preachers Conference. During a coffee break, I spoke with my pastor. I remarked that I wasn't creative. He immediately told me, "Don't say that about yourself. You create with words." His encouragement was an "Aha!" moment for me that I will always be grateful for.

***And we know that God causes everything to work together for the good of those who love God and are called according to his purpose for them* (Romans 8:28 NLT).**

Throughout the years I have learned much about creativity from online communities, the knowledge and wisdom of teachers and mentors at writers conferences, and simply being a part of a family of creatives. We have a few writers, digital artists, and even a baker! I marvel at the inspiration of God working through each of us as we collaborate and walk with him in his purpose for our lives. Going back to school has been another way for me to tap into creativity by taking writing-specific courses and honing my skills as God grows and increases this beautiful gift. It is an honor to spend the time he allows composing messages that point back to Him with the words he has given me.

For since the creation of the world God's invisible qualities—his eternal power and divine nature—have been clearly seen, being understood from what has been made, so that people are without excuse **(Romans 1:20 NIV).**

This verse reminds me that God shares his creativity with us. His invisible qualities, eternal power, and divine nature are clearly seen in us as we choose to allow him to work through us.

I am thankful for the worldwide platform God gives me and all creatives to share the good news of the gospel in all his many and various ways. As I loosen my grip on the work, he opens my eyes to new social media opportunities.

Staying consistently tethered to Jesus helps me to continually understand what his creativity looks like in my life. This encourages me forward in using and sharing this gift with others.

23

Mom, It's Ugly! A Child's Parable

by Ellie Langford

"Yuck! Mom. There's an ugly blob of bird poop on this leaf." Amelia loved helping Mom keep the butterfly garden beautiful. "I'll take the leaf off and put it in the trash."

"Wait. Let me look at it," said Mom.

"Why? It's gross!"

Mom walked over and gently poked it.

"It moved! It's alive," exclaimed Amelia. "Ohhh, two scary red horns just came out."

"What looks like horns is a part of the caterpillar's defense," said Mom.

"It's a strange caterpillar. Phew! It smells awful," said Amelia.

"That smell's coming from those 'horns.'"

"It looks nasty, has scary red horns, and stinks," complained Amelia. "Besides that, it's ugly. Do we have to let it stay in our beautiful garden?"

"God can take something ugly and change it into something beautiful. This caterpillar will become a more colorful caterpillar and form a chrysalis. Inside the chrysalis, it will go through amazing changes. It will come out of the chrysalis as a lovely Giant Swallowtail butterfly."

"A Giant Swallowtail! Mom, we can't let anything hurt this caterpillar."

"We'll do our best to help it become a butterfly," said Mom. "And our 'bird poop visitor' will do its part. But it's God's creative, marvelous plan that will cause it to become a beautiful butterfly."

"I can hardly wait," said Amelia.

24

Dear Jesus: A Child's Prayer

by Ellie Langford

Dear Jesus,

There are so many things I love about you.

You created a beautiful world

full of gifts for us:

family,

friends,

pets,

strawberries and watermelon,

and so much more.

But sadly, some people messed up the world,

and still do.

People did bad and mean things,

and still do.

You came down from heaven

to show us you still loved us.

You helped the poor.

You healed the sick

and comforted the sad.

Jesus, you taught us how to live.

You took the punishment
for all our bad choices
and died so we could be forgiven.
I'm glad you didn't stay dead.
You came back to life. Wow!
And then you went up to heaven.
But first you promised to come back
and get us so we can be with you.
You also promised
to create a beautiful world again
for those who love you.
I can hardly wait to hug you.
It's true, Jesus; there are so many things
I love about you.
But the very best thing,
I love about you,
is that you love me.
Amen.

Meet the Authors

Dian Avila

Dian and her husband, Jose, spent 10 years serving in missions overseas with their three children. They now live in South San Jose, California. Jose continues to travel throughout Latin America as a missionary. Dian delights in spending time with her three adult children, two sons-in-law, and four grandchildren. She also enjoys encouraging others as an assistant principal at Legacy Christian School.

Terese Belme

Terese's passion is to come alongside others and encourage them in their identity, authority, and inheritance in Jesus as ambassadors to the kingdom of God. Terese is a contributing author to the anthologies *Inspire Love* (2017) and *Inspire Kindness* (2018). Terese lives in the lower Pacific Northwest.

Terrie Hellard-Brown

Terrie Hellard-Brown is a writer, speaker, and podcaster. Her podcasts are *Books that Spark* and *Everyday Discipleship Every Day*. Her books include *Building Character through Picture Books* and *A World of Pancakes*. Her writing appears in Starlight Magazine, Upper Room, and in Inspire Christian Writers anthologies and on their blog.

Debra Celovsky

Debra Celovsky has served in pastoral ministry most of her adult life. Her devotionals and articles have appeared in a number of publications. She is on the board of Inspire Christian Writers and oversees compilation of the annual Inspire Anthology. Debra is partial to the One Year Bible, her grandchildren, and good conversation. Debra enjoys blogging and her work can be found at www.debracelovsky.com.

Carlitta Cole-Kelly

Carlitta is a writer, crafter, and genealogy enthusiast who enjoys creating short non-fiction and devotionals. Her work has appeared in several magazines, and she has one self-published children's book, *A Christmas Conversation: The Day Jesus Visited Santa*. She holds a B.S.N. from California State University, Bakersfield, and a M.A. from William Jessup University.

Laura Dorsey

Laura and her husband, Vance, live in Northern California with their seven children, whom they've homeschooled for over twenty years. Laura is published in the *Inspire Love* anthology.

Christine Hagion

Christine Hagion writes poems, songs, blogs, plays, articles, and books. An ordained minister, she has counseled abuse victims and survivors for over twenty years. "Dr. Red" (her nickname) specializes in raising awareness in the Christian Church about the issue of family violence, and the ability to heal from trauma.

Michala Hampton

Michala Hampton is a daydreamer caught between the worlds she brings to life in her stories and the one called "reality." When she's not writing, Michala is searching for opportunities to satisfy her wanderlust, trying new foods to appease her Hobbit appetite, and gathering story inspirations.

Joyce D. Hightower

Dr. Joyce D. Hightower, author, songwriter, and speaker, has always loved sharing stories. Her works reveal a trove of world experiences. These include international and local medical careers, raising three children as a single mother, and founding an international non-profit supporting orphans and widows.

<u>Debbie Jones-Warren</u>

Debbie writes memoir about her childhood in a boarding school in Nigeria where her parents were missionaries. Her devotions and short stories are published in The Upper Room, Chicken Soup for the Soul, and, in addition to Inspire, various other anthologies. She leads a writers group in the Bay Area. Read Debbie's blog at www.debbiejoneswarren.com.

<u>Ellie Langford</u>

Ellie is a Christian mom, teacher, and author. She has helped develop science books used in schools nationwide, and her stories have appeared in Christian magazines. Ellie won first place in a Tennessee Mountain Writers Contest and an Honorable mention in a Writer's Digest contest. She is a member of The Society of Children's Book Writers and Illustrators, and Children's Book Insider.

<u>Lainey La Shay</u>

Lainey La Shay is a writer who shines light on the deep issues of life and relationships, and wants to bring hope to her readers who are facing insurmountable odds. She is the author of the devotional journal *More Than a Survivor* and writes for Focus on the Family. La Shay is a member of American Christian Fiction Writers, Inspire Christian Writers, Pikes Peak Writers, Cascade Christian Writers, and Women's Fiction Writers of America.

Maureen Miller

Maureen Miller is an award-winning author who lives in western North Carolina with her husband, Bill, and their teenage daughter. She enjoys life in all its forms and looks for God's extraordinary character in the ordinary of life. Her first novel, *Gideon's Book*, is scheduled for release later in 2024.

Robyn Mulder

Robyn Mulder lives in South Dakota with her husband, Pastor Gary Mulder. Their four children and two grandchildren all live in Lincoln, Nebraska. Robyn writes about faith, productivity, and mental health at www.robynmulder.com. In 2024, she published her first book, *Staying Away from the Edge.*

Christopher Myers

Christopher loves writing, talking, and learning about how God engages in our lives. Published stories include *Grandpop's Trunk* in the Florida Writers Association 2023 Anthology, *Who Would Have Thought* in Clubfoot Connections, and *Start from Zero*, his blog & faith column for the St. Augustine Record.

Kimberly Novak

Kimberly Novak is a writer, spiritual director, and secretary who strives to inspire and uplift people on their spiritual path. She adores butterflies and is on a mission to spread the light of Christ through various ministries. For Kimberly's writings and her book, *Bella's Beautiful Miracle,* visit www.kimberlynovak.com.

Susan Sage

Susan Sage is a writer, mentor, blogger, speaker, and teacher who uses every opportunity to encourage someone else's heart. She is especially passionate about nurturing women to connect deeply with God. She blogs at www.susansage.com.

Libby Taylor-Worden

Libby has been a writer for many years. She recently added fiction to her background in magazine, non-fiction, anthology, journalism, devotionals, and curriculum. She lives in northern California with her husband and four-legged fur-baby.

Adrienne N. Wartts

Adrienne is an editor, writer, and photographer. Her articles have appeared in David C. Cook Ministries' *Power for Living,* Our Daily Bread Ministries' *VOICES,* and Hallmark's *Mahogany* blog. Her full-length collection of spiritual reflections is scheduled for release in 2025. Adrienne enjoys bird watching, traveling, cooking, and spending time with her family and pets.

About Inspire Christian Writers

Inspire Christian Writers is a nonprofit organization that exists to encourage and equip writers. ICW has members across the United States and in multiple countries. What began as a simple writing group in California has developed into a comprehensive organization meeting the needs of writers in numerous ways:

- Our award-winning blog and website (named a top ten worldwide blog and website resource for Christian writers)
- Online critique groups for various genres
- Online workshops
- Directory of vetted professionals serving writers
- Networking opportunities
- Annual anthology to showcase our members' work
- Writing credits via our blog and anthology

If you are interested in joining Inspire, or want information on our current events and offerings, visit www.inspirewriters.com. We look forward to welcoming you!

Previous Anthologies from Inspire Christian Writers

Inspire Trust (2012)

Inspire Faith (2013)

Friends of Inspire Faith (2013)

Inspired Glimpses of God's Presence (2013)

Inspire Victory (2014)

Inspire Promise (2014)

Inspire Forgiveness (2015)

Inspire Joy (2016)

Inspire Love (2017)

Inspire Kindness (2018)

Inspire Grace (2019)

Inspire Community (2021

Inspire Courage (2022)

Inspire Honor (2023)

Made in the USA
Las Vegas, NV
06 December 2024

13477693R00069